Copyright © 2022 Clavis Publishing Inc., New York

Visit us on the Web at www.clavis-publishing.com.

A Better Way to Bell a Cat written by Bonnie Grubman and illustrated by Judi Abbot

ISBN 978-1-60537-766-7

This book was printed in March 2022 at Nikara, M. R. Štefánika 858/25, 963 01 Krupina, Slovakia.

First Edition
10 9 8 7 6 5 4 3 2 1

Written by Bonnie Grubman
Illustrated by Judi Abbot

A BETTER WAY TO BELL A CAT

Clavis

NEW YORK

Elwood, Bernardo, and Vincent lived
a pleasant life in the big old house . . . until
the humans brought home a rather large tabby.
MEOW!
"EEEK," gasped Bernardo.
"Start packing," shrilled Elwood, as the cat
came barrelling down the cellar stairs.

"Whew. That was close," whispered Vincent.
"We're doomed," wheezed Bernardo.
"Maybe not," said Vincent.
Maybe not? thought Elwood,
shrinking into a corner.

"I have an idea," suggested Vincent.
"Let's tie a bell around the cat's neck.
It will jingle and warn us when the cat is approaching."
"And give us time to escape," added Bernardo.
Vincent and Bernardo waited for Elwood's reaction.
"B-but who will bell the cat?" stammered Elwood.
No one volunteered.

So, Vincent came up with something else,
and when the coast was clear, they acted quickly.

"How long do we have to stay like this?" asked Bernardo.
"Till the cat comes back and loses interest," said Vincent.

But Elwood got dizzy too soon.

"Oh rats," said Bernardo. "Now what?"
"I'll knit some sweaters," said Elwood.
"KNIT?" snapped Bernardo.
"We're going to need them when we're homeless."

"Homeless shmomeless," quipped Vincent.
"Remember the old fable about the lion
that was captured in a hunter's net?"
Where is he going with this? thought Elwood.
"A brave little mouse gnawed on the ropes
and freed the grateful lion. What if our cat
found itself in a similar situation?"
"It might spare our lives too," said Elwood with hope.

So, when the cat curled up for a nap, the mice raided
the knitting basket and quickly got to work.

But Elwood got hives from the itchy wool
and quit before they could properly trap
the cat, much less come to its rescue.
"Sorry, guys," sighed Elwood.

The mice took one last look
at the place they called home.
"Goodbye forever, Fluffy," whimpered Elwood.
"We'll miss you," said Bernardo.

Vincent gazed at the plush dog.
"Wait," he blurted.
He'd had another brainstorm.

"Mark my words," Vincent bragged.
"The cat will run for the hills."
"It's preposterous," said Elwood.
"But brilliant," said Bernardo.

So, when the cat curled up for another nap, Vincent squeezed
through the rip on Fluffy's belly. "How do I look, guys?"
"How should we know? We can't see you."
"That's the point. Now join me
in the performance of our lives."

The mice tiptoed to the cat's ear.

WOOF!

WOOF!

WOOF!

But the cat didn't run for the hills.
"Nice disguise, guys."
"H-how d-did you know?" spluttered Elwood.
"For one thing, you can't bark
to save your lives, and besides,
who ever heard of a pink dog?"
A long silence filled the room.

"So, what are you going to do with us?" asked Vincent.

"Nothing. I'm not a mouser.

I'm just a cat who fancies canned food,

friendship, and harmonious living."

"Why didn't you say so?" cried Elwood.

"You didn't give me a chance."

One by one, the mice inched out.

"Welcome to your new home," they squeaked.

The new housemates shared furry tales and laughed their heads off over catnip and crumbs. Life was purr-fect in the big old house . . . until the humans brought home a rather large pup.

AESOP'S FABLES